P9-DXN-059

LUZ
MAKES a
SPLASH

Kids Can Press acknowledges the financial support of the Government of Ontario, through the Ontario Media Development Corporation's Ontario Book Initiative; the Ontario Arts Council; the Canada Council for the Arts; and the Government of Canada, through the BPIDP, for our publishing activity.

Published in Canada by
Kids Can Press Ltd.
25 Dockside Drive
Toronto, ON M5A 0B5

Published in the U.S. by
Kids Can Press Ltd.
2250 Military Road
Tonawanda, NY 14150

www.kidscanpress.com

Edited by Karen Li and Samantha Swenson
Designed by Claudia Dávila and Rachel Di Salle

The hardcover edition of this book is
smyth sewn casebound.
The paperback edition of this book is
limp sewn with a drawn-on cover.
Manufactured in Shen Zhen, Guang Dong,
P.R. China, in 5/2012 by Printplus Limited.

CM 12 0 9 8 7 6 5 4 3 2 1
CM PA 12 0 9 8 7 6 5 4 3 2 1

Library and Archives Canada Cataloguing in Publication

Dávila, Claudia
Luz makes a splash / by Claudia Dávila.

ISBN 978-1-55453-762-4 (bound) ISBN 978-1-55453-769-3 (pbk.)

I. Title. II. Series: Dávila, Claudia. Future according to Luz.

PS8607.A95285L87 2012 jC813'.6 C2011-906930-X

Kids Can Press is a Corus™ Entertainment company

LUZ
MAKES a
SPLASH
By
Claudia
Dávila
Kids Can Press

For Michael and Yolanda

Contents

... the hottest summer on record here in Petroville. Everyone's feeling the heat, but the young and elderly are at greatest risk for heatstroke in what's being called a record-breaking drought ...
Whrrrrr
rr.......

GZZLR

WELCOME TO Paradise MALL
Well, there goes the last of my allowance.
But it's SO worth it, Anika!
Besides, what choice do we have? It's either eating ice cream in air conditioning or melting into a puddle of sweat outside!
?
Uh-oh. Looks like we're gonna need a new plan. Look, Luz!
We're helping the environment!
Scheduled brownouts daily
11 am – 12 pm
We apologize for any inconvenience.
Signed,
Management
Paradise Mall

BEAT the HEAT

We've gotta think of something. It's only morning and I'm already baking!
Paradise
Is it just me, or is the sidewalk reflecting heat right at my face?
No, you're right. All this concrete makes it feel like we're in an oven!
We need water.
How about the pool?
Or better yet ...
SPRING POND!
Oh! Good thinking!
Robert has to come, too.

I don't think he's ever been there before.
ding!
Aw yeah, Spring Pond ...
Hey, guys! What's up?
Your *sweater* is what's up! Don't you know it's a heat wave out there?
Heh! Not in here.
Holy cow! It's freezing!
You're here by yourself — and the whole house is air conditioned?
Hey, it works for me.
Luz, **shh!**

I'm sorry, but that's just crazy!
Hey! What are you doing?
Consider it your little contribution to the environment.
Besides, we're taking you to the watering hole just outside of town. You can cool off naturally!
You might want to leave your sweater here.
And I have to ask my mom.
Let's go, Anika!
Do we have to?

SOON AFTER ...
So explain to me again why going to a pond is better than staying cool at home?
It's actually really nice! It's always cold because a spring fills it up.
I saw a family of ducks once. So cute!
It's deep enough to go swimming ...
... and it's surrounded by trees! My mom and I used to go all the time when I was little.
I hate swimming.
Aw, you'll like it!
We're here!

It's just through here!
I'm not hearing any ducks quacking.

I am not swimming in *that*.
This is so weird.
I'm sure we didn't get off at the wrong stop. This should be Spring Pond!
More like Dead Pond.
It's like it dried up. Do you think it ... evaporated? You know, because of the heat wave?
I don't know ... but this is bad! And I bet those ducks are feeling the heat even more than we are.
Good point. Can we go now? This is an epic drag.

What do we do now?
I'm thirsty.
PROPERTY OF
TOP COLA
The Only Cola Made with Fresh Spring Water!
Hey, look!
Now that's what I'm talking about! A nice cold soft drink.
That sign wasn't here before. And see what it says? "Made with fresh spring water."
The spring that used to fill this pond?

That's what I think! That company took all the water, and now it's all dried up!
Pond water — in soft drinks? Okay, that's gross.
Ugh.
Wait, look at those pipes! They aren't going to the pond, they're going into the *ground*.
But I don't get it. There's no water over there.

BACK IN THE CITY ...
What are you guys going to do now?
The only thing I can do to cool off — take a cold shower!
And I have a nice, cool house waiting for me.
Y-you guys are welcome to come over. If you want.
Nah, a shower sounds good to me. Catch you guys later.
See ya.

¡Hola, Abuela!
Abuela? Are you okay?
MOM! Come quick!
¡Ai, niña! You don't have to shout.
Luz, what's wrong?
I am all right. Just need some agua.

Did you pass out?
This heat is too much for your grandma.
I already said I am fine.
But, Luz — why are you covered in mud?
Oh! I went down to the pond with Robert and Anika. It's all mucky there now. You know, it's almost all dried up!
What do you mean, *dried up*?
Well, I'm not positive, but I think Top Cola sucked up all the water.
¿Qué?
There was a sign saying they own the property. I think they used the pond's spring to make soft drinks.
Ai, no. Not here, too.
Huh?
This happened in our homeland. A mining company bought land and pumped water out of the ground. Many people suffered without clean water.

People got sick? I thought it was bad enough the birds and fish lost their homes.
This is terrible.
We have to do something!
Hang on, chica, first we need to make sure we know what's really going on.
I'm going to call city council and our local Sierra Club. If what you say is true, we're going to boycott Top Cola!
¡Amén!
WHAT?! Isn't that a bit ... extreme?
... I like their soft drinks.

Come, Luz. Let's get Abuela some ice tea.
Okay. But first I really need to take a shower. I'm hot and muddy!
NOTICE
CITY-WIDE WATER RESTRICTIONS IN EFFECT
That shower's going to have to wait. We got a notice from the city that water will be turned off during the day.
Oh, groan! WHY?
To conserve water. I'm guessing it's because of this drought.
Can this day get any worse?

LATER THAT AFTERNOON ...
junebug café
Maybe it's not as hot in the park.
junebug café
Hi, Luz!
Market Today
Hi, Mrs. Kim! How is your basil this week?
Ah, thirsty. And we're not allowed to water our plants with this new city ban ...
NOTICE
CITY-WIDE WATER RESTRICTIONS IN EFFECT
COMMUNITY GARDENS
Mmm, it *is* a little cooler here with these trees.

How can I sell these shriveled little tomatoes? They're barely fit for compost!
And without rain, how are we supposed to water our gardens? All our plants are going to wilt and die.
Face it, we need to conserve water and use less of it. It's only logical.
We can't use less, Gord. We need more! My lawn is turning brown, and my car needs a wash real bad.
You still drive a car? Trade it in for a bike, Sunil. Times are changing!

Sigh.
We put too much work into Friendship Park to just let it dry out.
But can the Farmers' Market go on?
The water ban is killing our crops.
I can't fill my swimming pool. My kids need it!
And who are they to restrict our water?
glug glug
Yeah, let's just ignore the rules!

Nah, Gord's right. We can't use what little water there is. We'll just run out sooner.
Then we have to get water from somewhere else.
But where?
Hey! The city should build a pipeline from the pond just outside the city. There's lots of water there!

But what about the fish and frogs that need that water?
And what happens when we've used up the pond? We'll be right where we started, or worse!
Besides, that pond is almost empty now.
I was just there. Top Cola has bought the property.
W-what are you saying?
And now Spring Pond is just a mud pit.

What does this mean, Mom?
They're taking the spring's water to make — canned soft drinks?
This is outrageous!
A giant textiles company did that in my homeland, too. Not only did our town end up with no water, the company pumped out polluted waste, too!

But I love Top Cola. They wouldn't do something like that!
My mom's checking it out. If it's true, we're going to boycott their products to protest what they're doing.
That's a great idea. But it's not enough. We need to tell that company we want the pond restored!
That doesn't solve our problems here in the city. We still need water!
We just have to pray for rain.

No pond, no soft drinks, no water ... no peace!
This is going to be a long summer.

EVERY DROP COUNTS

Yes!
Rain is coming!
Come on, rain ...

I can almost taste it!
Wha —?!
Ack! This is too much!
So close, and yet so far ...
It hasn't rained in three weeks!
I'm going to wash my face, if that's all right with the authorities!

Oh!
... Here are other communities that have filed complaints against Top Cola ...
Hi, Luz.
'Morning.
Let's look for other cases of water rights abuses around the world.

Okay, gotta go!
Wait ... what are you guys up to?
Can't talk now. Robert's waiting for me. We're going to make posters together!
We're working on a letter to Top Cola.
We need to campaign against them draining the groundwater and wrecking Spring Pond.
We're also starting an online petition. We want to get this from every angle!

Oh! Right. Sounds like a good plan.
Es muy malo. These companies can't keep hurting people and nature.
You're working on this, too, Abuela?
Sí, I want to help.
You need to rest and keep cool, Mamá. We've got this covered.
Well ... maybe I can help, too?
Tsk!

I said, I'd like to help!
Oh, Luz, we're fine. You go out and have fun. Go play with your friends or something.
Go play? How old does she think I am?
Besides, my friends are too busy to "play" with me ...

SOON AFTER ...
NOTICE
Sigh.
NOTICE
CITY WIDE
WATER
RESTRICTIONS
IN EFFECT
Hello, Luz!
Oh, hi, Mr. DeSouza! What's with all the pickles?
GARLIC
PICKLES
This isn't pickles anymore! It's empty. I'm going to use it to catch rain.

There! That's a good spot.
For catching rain?
Exactly! Rain falls on the roof and then pours into the eaves troughs. From there, it goes down the pipe and ...
See, this is the problem. It washes into the street and down the sewer. Wasted! So the solution is —
Oh! To catch it!
The barrel goes under the pipe. After just an hour of rain, it'll be full. I could water my plants for a week!
Cool! But there's one problem.
No rain.

But we need to be prepared, or these plants haven't got a chance!
Everyone at Friendship Park sure is worried because they can't water their gardens.
Mm, yes ...
Oh, good, you're setting up the rain barrel!
Sí, sí, it's almost ready.
Hi, Mrs. DeSouza!
Hello, Luz. How is your grandma in all this heat?
I hope she's doing better than my roses ...

This is why we need the barrels, fast! My flowers need a lot of water.
But with this drought and the water ban, they won't survive the summer!
Wow, even your corn and vegetables look sad, Mrs. D.
I wonder how plants can grow in the wild without people watering them all the time!
Ah, that's because of groundwater.

In nature, there is always water deep underground. Rivers and streams trickle into the soil along with rainwater.

It spreads all over, and plants can drink it up through their roots to keep healthy and growing.

So plants get watered by rain above, as well as from below!

But in the city, there's very little groundwater — instead, we have basements and subways and sewers.

When it rains, water can't land on the soil because buildings and roads cover the ground! Rain is lost into sewer pipes.

So if you don't have rain, and you don't have groundwater, the only way to get water to your plants is to do it yourself.
And that's why Spring Pond is all dried up — the groundwater is getting sucked dry by the cola factory!
Nothing from above and nothing from below.
Sigh. So it is.

Mr. D. is doing a great thing. But it's only for his little yard.
Our whole city needs help!
Good morning, Mrs. Kim! How is your harvest today?
But what can I do about it?
!

Hi, you guys!
Hey!
Where to next?
Oh, forget them!

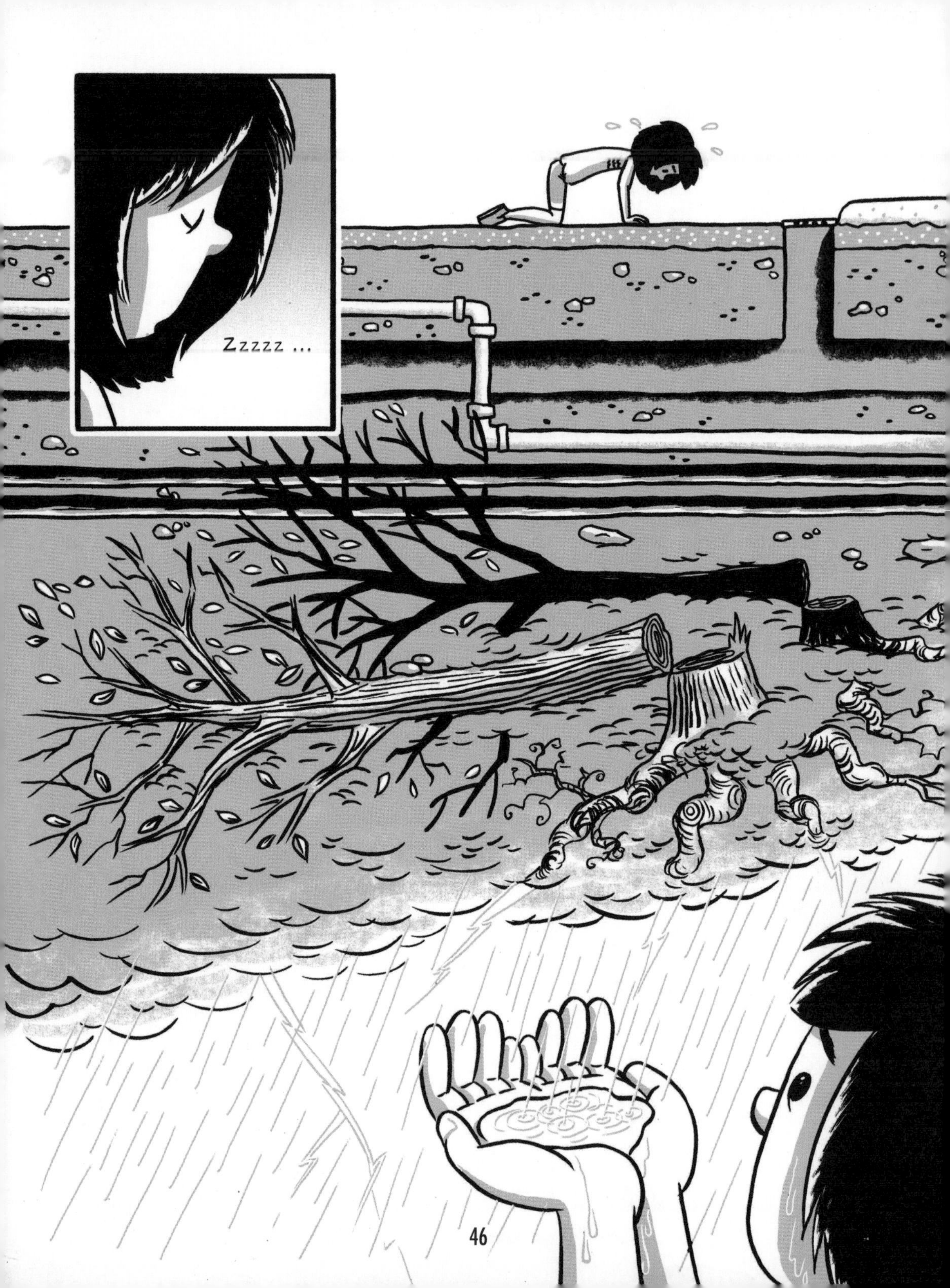
Zzzzz ...

SPLASH!

What was *that?!*
SPLASH!
STOP! Y-you can't do that!
Huh?
I *mean*, we're in a drought, and that's perfectly good water you're throwing out.
Oh, *sorry*, did you want to *drink it* or something? It's only mop water!
Hi, Luz. What's the problem, guys?

The plants — I mean, these gardens — we need that mop water — like, that's *wasting water* ...
Oh, *ack!*
I don't understand.
No kidding.
What I'm trying to say is, why are you *throwing out* water when there's a shortage?
But, Luz, this isn't fresh water. Our café needs lots of water, for cleaning and food and laundry ... what do you expect us to do with it after we use it?

Well, I don't know.
But these gardens are drying out.
Mrs. Kim's herbs are dying. They
need water from somewhere!
I'm sorry, but I can't do
anything about that.
This is
wastewater,
like you said.
"Waste?"
So what do you
want me to do
with this?
Just dump it,
I guess.

Gord always says that in nature there's no such thing as —
SPLASH!
— waste!
Heya, Luz!
Hi ...?
Oh, you must be wondering what all this awesome stuff is for, if it isn't obvious already.

I'm building
a graywater
filtration system,
yeah!
Gord, you're doing it again! Can
you talk in people speak, *please?*
I'm talking about the answer to
our water shortage problems!
Then you'd need to
build a rain maker ...
Tried that, didn't work. But
seriously, there is only one
real problem with water.
What
is it?
I'll tell you
what it is.

WASTE!
We waste rain by draining it into our sewers. We waste groundwater by using too much of it, for things we don't need.
And we waste tap water by only using it once.
Yeah, I get it. Mr. D. told me how we can catch rain —
— and you saw how Top Cola drained groundwater for soft drinks — it's a waste!
But what can we do with tap water?

A-ha!
That's where my graywater filtration system comes in!
Tap water is good for drinking, cooking, bathing, washing ...
After it's used once, it's called graywater. But it can be used again!
MOP BUCKET!

?
Mop bucket??
Ha-ha! Look out, June! Your wastewater is actually graywater!
Right, not to be confused with *blackwater*, which is used toilet water.
Though I think that should be called *brownwater* —
Ew!
Don't even go there, Gord!
Holy cow. I just had an idea.
We have to talk to Mr. D.!

... So the graywater pours into a contalner full of gravel and marsh plants. And the water that comes out is clean!
It sounds so simple!
GRAY WATER
NATURAL FILTER
CLEAN WATER
Mr. D., we have got a brilliant plan to save Friendship Park, and we need YOU!
Hello, Luz. Hiya, Gord.
Oh?

Look, look! Gord can set up a way to use wastewater, and you know how to use rainwater, so between the two of you —
— we can irrigate all the plants! Luz, that's really smart.
I've got lots of barrels we can use in the park. Hmm ...
We need to put in eaves troughs, and for that, we need awnings!
Oof!
There are no roofs in the park, but we need a surface to catch the water — and shade!
Lots to do ...

Let's get to work on these rain barrels!
Um, Mr. DeSouza?
Can I help?
You're always helping, Luz.

BOILING POINT
GARDENS

Yeah, that's looking real good, Luz!
Thanks, Mr. D.! I think this is the last one to do.
Heh-heh! Well, after two weeks of lots of work by lots of people, I think this water system is almost ready.

Yup! We got the awnings, eaves troughs and barrels. And the hoses can reach all the garden plots.
WINDOW
STAGE
MINI MARSH
RAIN BARREL
ROOF WITH EAVES TROUGH
HOSE
RAIN BARRELS
GAZEBO WITH EAVES TROUGH
All that's missing is the "mini marsh" ...
... the bathtub!
For the graywater filter?
But where will the water come from?
Junebug Café uses lots of water every day.
The laundry can automatically drain into the mini marsh through a hose. Easy!

So what have you guys been doing out here?
Hey, June! Don't you know? We're building a water-saving system to help keep the gardens alive — and you have a big part to play!
I do? Really? How exciting!
Ooh, and that means more basil and tomatoes for the café!
Oh, this is very good news.
You and your friends are so clever!
Hmph! "Friends." What friends?

It's been weeks since I've seen Robert and Anika.
What are they up to, anyway?
HAVE YOU SEEN SPRING POND?
Raise your voices against corporations destroying ecosystems and depleting our water!
SIGN THE ONLINE PETITION

KNOCK KNOCK KNOCK!
please knock! no doorbell during blackout
Why do I bother.
He's probably hanging out with my best friend and eating ice cream and playing video games and ... and ...

LATER ...
Hrk!
H-help? Anyone?
Gord!
Hang on!
Holy cow, Gord! Wasn't there an easier way to do this?
We need reinforcements — HELP!!
Woah!
Here we go!
HEAVE!
Whew! Thanks, everybody!
Pant! Pant!

I think ... pant, pant! ... I just need ... a little rest!
Oh, is this for me?
YES! You can put your wastewater in this tub now instead of throwing it out!
Excellent — back in a flash!
That's right, Luz! Because in nature there's no such thing as —

—waAAAGH!
I *just* washed some apples.
EEK! That's not what I meant!!

We still need to turn this tub into a mini marsh! Once we connect the hoses, we'll use graywater from your *laundry*!
Great, now I smell like apples.
Well, at least it's refreshing!
So sorry. Here!
Hey!
honk honk

Honk!
Hey, Luz! Grab your stuff, and get in!
We're going to Top Cola.
We've got a letter of protest and a copy of our online petition for them.
Come with us!
You don't need me for that. Besides, there's no room in the car.

Yank!
Hey!
Shove!
Flump!
Slam!
Everybody ready to go?
No!
YES!
Let's check on the pond first.
You know, Dad, we could have taken the bus!
Oh! Well, maybe, yeah ...

SOON AFTER ...
Oh ... my ... goodness.
What happened?!

Where are you going?
Dad, we're too late!

I care, too, you know. Maybe I could have saved you — if they had let me help.
Oh, you're so parched ... you're just going to dry out here.

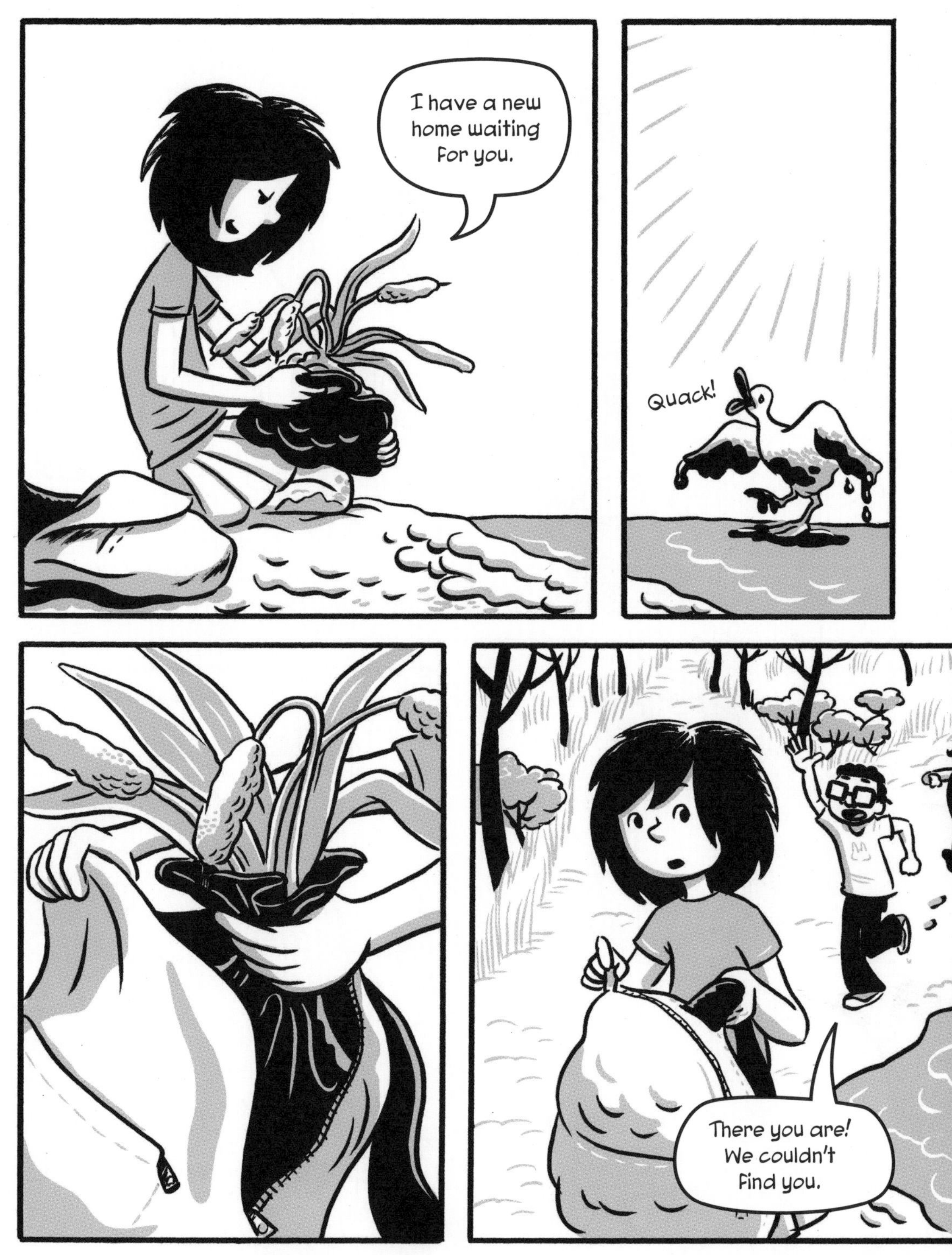
I have a new home waiting for you.
Quack!
There you are! We couldn't find you.

Yeah, right. Like you even noticed I was gone.
Luz, we've been busy!
Dad said he needed our help — it's a lot of work campaigning against a big corporation!
Well, maybe I wanted to help!
We thought you'd be *happy* we were doing something important. Like *you* always do!
What are you talking about?

Robert's right. You care about important things. You make things *happen*.
Like Friendship Park!
W-what?
What you did was amazing. The park would never have happened without you.
Oh!
Wow.
But ...
But you're wrong. I couldn't have done it without *you*. I need you guys. And this whole summer, you've made me feel like you didn't need *me*.

Let's make a promise.
From now on, we work together. As a team!
Yeah!
For real?
We need you, too, Luz!
Team handshake!
Together!
We're a team!
SPLAK!
Hey!

Ha
Ha
Ha
Ha
Ha
Ha
Ha
SPLOOCH
Come on, kids. We're leaving. ¡Vamos!
Bye!
See ya!
Mom, I just have to go do something. Back soon.
Okay, chica.

afé
Hey, Gord set up the mini marsh!
I hope these gardens have better luck than Spring Pond.
Enjoy your new home, little reeds.

Muy bien, chica. Very nice.
Hm?
Abuela! What are you doing here?
I'm handing out flyers about the Spring Pond mess.
I told you I'd do my part.
Aw, I'm sorry, Abuela ... but we just went to the pond. It's all dried up. It's too late to do anything about it.
Luz, it's never too late. We keep trying — *especially* if it feels like there's nothing more we can do.

A WEEK LATER ...
Whrr!
Whrr!
Whrr!
Swsssssh!
Splip
plip
plip
Gurgle
gurgle
Gurgle
gurgle
So cool.
gurgle
gurgle

Hi, Mrs. Kim! How's it going?
See for yourself! June's laundry water brought my plants back to life.
Mmm! It couldn't happen without the mini marsh, though.
Oh, yes!
Looks like we might get rain, too. We need it, after almost a month and a half of drought ...
Rain? I'll believe it when I see it.

Luz! Come quick, we gotta go to Robert's place!
Hi, Anika. What's up?
A team meeting about the pond! *Together*, remember?
Ack!
Oh, man, don't make me run! Don't you know how hot it is?
Wait, I forgot to bring a sweater.
Ha-ha!
No, I'm serious!

Come downstairs!
Hey, it's not cold!
Nah, after the last few brownouts, we thought we'd ease up on the A/C. You know, decrease our carbon fingerprint and all that.
Carbon Footprint!
Okay, check this out!
See this? "Top Cola has announced its Spring Pond Initiative. The company will slow production to help replenish groundwater levels ..."
"... It will also restore the pond habitat near its production plant by reintroducing fish, flora and fauna."

Our parents showed city hall the petition. It had thousands of names because of all our posters and flyers!

K-K-KRACK!
¡Ay!
What was that? Sounds like my house is breaking in half!
Thunder!
Think it's going to rain?
Nah. Probably just another tease. Dry thund —
K-K-KRACK!
SHHHHHH!

Yippee!!

OVERFLOW→

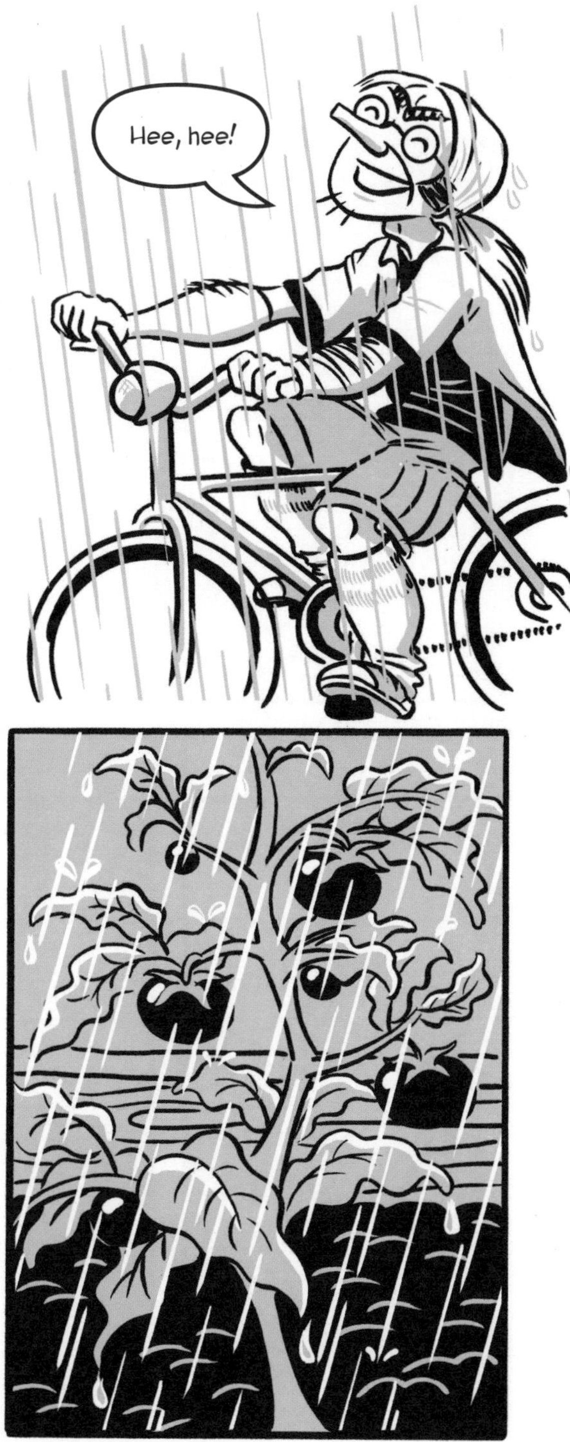
Hee, hee!

You made it,
little plants.

Abuela, we did it!
Yes, we did.

the END
QUACK!

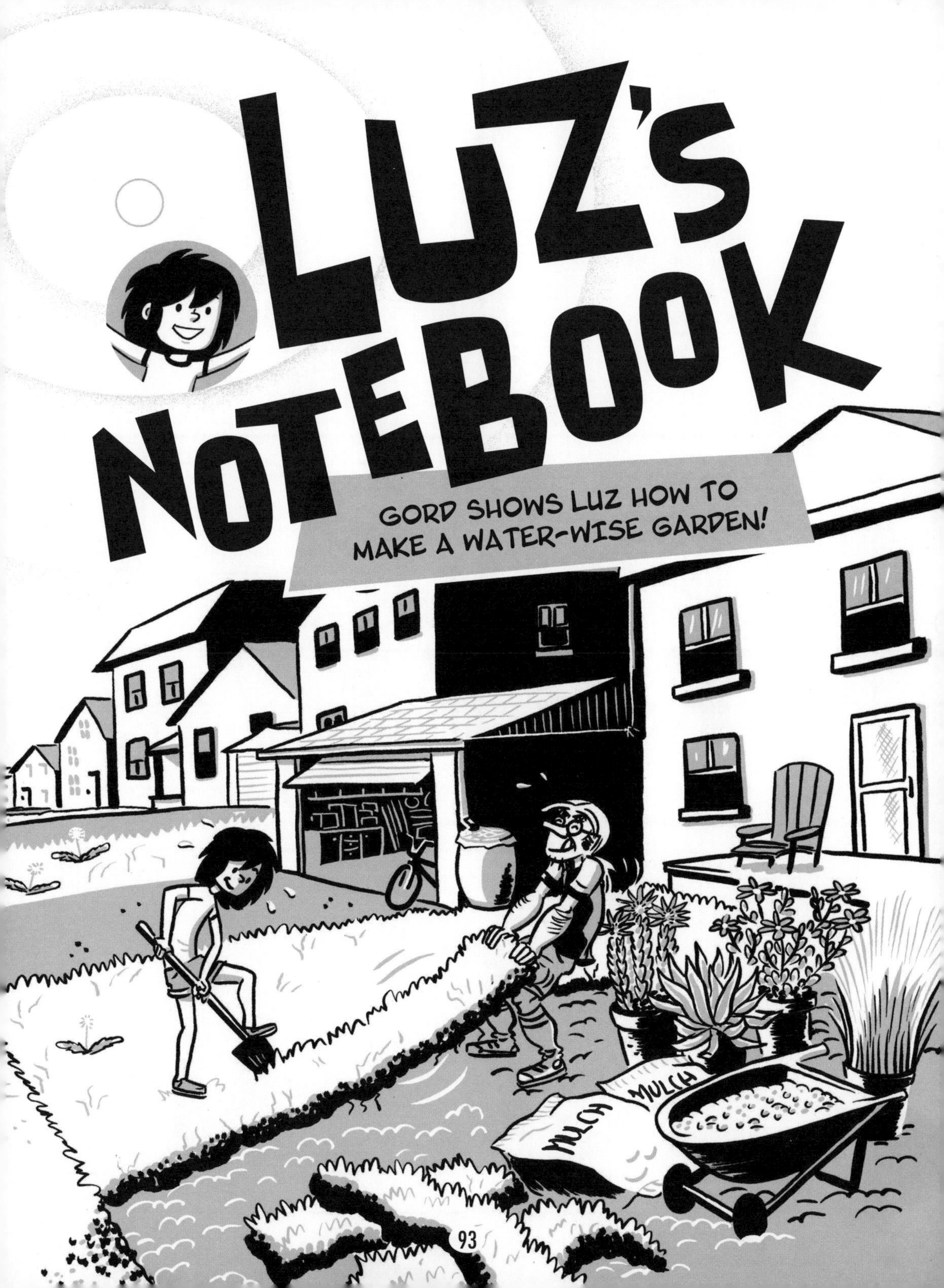
LUZ'S NOTEBOOK
GORD SHOWS LUZ HOW TO MAKE A WATER-WISE GARDEN!
MULCH
MULCH

Gord, you made your own mini marsh! Looking good.
Thanks, man. Now I can reuse gallons of graywater every day!
I assume it's for that sad patch of dead lawn?
Are you kidding? This is for my vegetable garden — lawns are useless! They use up too much precious water.
Eep!
Besides, I hate mowing. So let's tear it out!
What?
Gord, please tell me you know what you're doing.
What I'm doing is turning this into a rock garden full of sun-loving plants that don't need watering.
Drought? Water restrictions? No problem, we're xeriscaping!
ULCH

First we tear out the lawn and turn it into compost.
Now we break up the soil so it's loose enough for roots, air and water to get in.
Wherever the plants will go, we dump lots of rich compost.
Next we plop in our indigenous grasses and wildflowers.
Hello!
Then we cover the base with wood chips, and give everything a good watering.
Some decorative stones, pea gravel, and we're done!

Wow, Gord, this looks **way** better than a carpet of brown grass!
And I never have to mow it or water it!
And all these native plants mean we should see lots of —
Butterflies!
That's just ... beautiful!
Aw, Gord. You're such a softie!